The Blank Parchment

Allegra Vercesi

To all those ambitious kids out there.

♥

"As you grow older you will discover that you have two hands. One for helping yourself, the other for helping others."

-Audrey Hepburn

Chapter 1

❦

The beginning of it all

One-two-three-four…..one-two-three-four.

My ankles started to make crackling noises

and throb with pain.

The instructor had continued

….one-two-three-four ….. one-two-three-four.

The girl next to me dropped.

I kept going.

She called, "First position, second, third,

fourth, and fifth."

I started to catch my breath.

I felt at ease.

I had stopped sweating.

I remembered what I signed up for.

You see ballet was something I had always wanted to do!

I had a few lessons here and there until I was kicked out at the age of 6 because I was apparently "too aggressive with my arabesques."

Anyways that's beside the point:)

I restarted it as a hobby because mommy and daddy insisted on doing a sport.

Now I insist on introducing myself, shall I? Well, hello to whoever is reading this. My name is Constance. I know what you may be thinking, "what an odd name." I hate to break it to you, reader, but I like my name.

My parents are the Dutch and Duchess of Leonthuria, so that should answer your question about why my name is so complex.

I can attest to the fact that all royals name their kids something unique and add roman numerals at the end of their name to make it even more unique than the word unique itself.

One-two-three-four, she continued.

The instructor, Mariathonia, had finally ended the lesson.

I cannot believe I had just zoned out of that lesson, but hey, it helped me cope with the pain.

Anyways, back to me again. I am a sixteen-year-old girl and am an only child. I had always dreamt of having an older sister

to do ballet with and talk to. My parents,

whom I love very much, keep me very busy

though, so I don't have time for a sister! In

case you didn't know, my butler always has

my tutor accompany me to the music room

and play the piano. Just like he did today.

Just like every day. BUT it's not an issue

because I genuinely love to play and listen to

the piano, and have some company! There

truly is something so magical about the

piano. It is versatile. It fits every genre of

music if you know how to play it.

This reminds me of my outstanding

achievement, and that is that I recently

learned how to play a classical piece.

"Here you go, madam," Hobson said as he placed my cheese platter on the acrylic table.

"HOBSON, I ASKED FOR THAT PLATTER 20 MINUTES AGO" I yelled.

"Sor-" Hobson attempted to apologize.

"You are excused, leave" I said as I cut him off.

I stared at my piano tutor, raised my two eyebrows, and rolled my eyes.

I felt as if we were rudely interrupted, so I gracefully apologized to the tutor, and we continued.

Music calms me down. Not that I need to be calmed down. I am just used to getting what I want, when I want it, and how I want it.

AHHA immaculate! LADIES AND GENTLEMAN, introducing Constance's three w's (insert jazz hands here**). I have been told an awful amount of times that this trait in life will "do me justice." My best friend Anastasia has said that about 56 times. Fun fact that is the average count of my high heels as of Friday, October 10th. You see, I go on what my father calls "shopping sprees" every week. But that's hardly a good vocab word to describe such minuscule acts. I just go purchase shoes that match an outfit. I treat it like grocery shopping, charity work as a matter of fact. Nothing too glamorous about it. In reality, they are just shoes with a little extra height. No biggy.

Anyways back to the whole "life skills"

twaddle. On the other hand, multiple people

told me that I would fail if I "don't

compromise, especially in teamwork-related

job sectors."

Pfthhhht, the fact that people think I need to

work to sustain myself is funny. I had never

worked a day in my life, and I do not plan on

working a day in my life.

Some people may think what I said is too

harsh, and I want to just let you know that's

my personality, and there is nothing wrong

with it.

"Tutor, I have a question, which btw, has

nothing to do with reading a sheet of music."

I pouted my two lips, waiting for a response intently.

"Yes, I would be happy to answe-" she attempted to respond.

"UMMMM…so… I was wondering….if harsher is a word?"

"Well sweetie, I, uh, do not believe so."

"I thought you graduated from Harvard; you should be, like, smart," I remarked.

"I did, and I am," she stated.

"That was a rhetorical question, tutor."

"My apologies," she said in a highly strung voice.

I went back to playing the classical piece, and she applauded me on my music.

CLAP...CLAP...CLAP....I heard three

additional claps from the back of the room.

I immediately became anxious.

My eyebrows lifted, and I felt a strain

beneath my pupil, a burning sensation.

No one has ever heard me play piano before,

other than my tutor.

"Oh my, good job, sweetie!" My parents

exclaimed.

"Oh mamma, papa, hello! I did not know you

were here," I stated nervously.

My father gave the signal to the butler, who

escorted the tutor to the door.

"As always, thank you" He politely thanked

the tutor.

"Honey, we want you to try to go to an antique shop," My mom said as she rubbed my dad's back.

"We think you would really like it since you call yourself an "old soul" every hour of every day.

"Sorry, uh, Mom. Did you just say that **I, CONSTANCE ANDILET the second,** should go to an antique shop?"

"Ha-ha, ummm yes."

Mother commented as if she was uneasily walking on eggshells.

I let out a sigh and nodded my head.

"Really, are you sure? She asked.

"Mom, why are you asking so many questions? I said I will go, geez," I rolled my eyes

In all honesty, I just think she wants me out of the house.

It is not my fault my house is big enough never to have to leave it.

We have a grocery store on floor one.

A fitness room on the third floor.

A ballet room to practice in the east wing.

A music room underground.

A theatre on floor two.

A game room near the west wing.

A pool room near sunroom b.

A study room.

A couple of living rooms. A few kitchens.

And shall I continue…?

I understand where she is coming from, for once.

Chapter 2

❦

The Time Capsule

I waved to our chauffeur, who drove the limo to the front entrance. Mother and father decided it would be nice to purchase a limo with a white interior and grey exterior. That is so last season, like literally. Not to be a brat, but who will tell them that grey and white are outdated during the winter season. Sorry, not sorry. Like snow is white, the car just blends in. Last time I checked, we are humans and not chameleons!

A grand halt then followed up the screeching noise. We had come to a stop. I looked through the freshly cleaned window, and faced terror. Talk about PTSD. The last time I encountered something this horrid was when I was birthed. No one talks about the well-baby nursery room. If horrid needed a definition, that room would suffice. I felt a shiver down my back as I stepped out of the vehicle. He took me to this antique shop called "The Time Capsule."

I entered the store with bias and disgust. Reader, I hate to break it to you, but I am quite picky if you cannot tell. Like really picky. I saw some brown wooden figures, ugly clocks, dirty blankets, $5 jewelry, and postcards. The postcards attracted me though. I rushed to them. I stepped over a

couple of dog toys and blankets. My legs
crossed one another as I moved in a steady
direction browsing the postcards. My eyes
looked up, down, then left, to the right. I
stopped as I heard some commotion nearby. A
lady with white curly hair, creepy teeth, and
pretty blue eyes greeted me.
"Halleooooo," she uttered in a strained voice.
I simply smiled and waved at her and carried
on.
She tilted her head and proceeded to move
the pots and pans. She was throwing things
around.
These postcards were so cool, I thought to
myself.

"No, no, this is expired, NOOO, nope," she commented as she threw things carelessly in the invisible "no pile."

There were postcards from Paris, London, Dubai, and Indonesia! I remained somewhat awe-struck.

I gasped as I saw a piano with buckets and buckets of music sheets.

There was every classical piece of music any piano player could dream of ......☆♫○♩● ♪✧♩

♫☆ Beethoven: Bagatelle No

♫☆ Rachmaninov: 5 Morceaux de fantaisie Op

♫☆ Beethoven: Piano Sonata No

♫☆ Liszt: Liebesträume, S

♫☆ Liszt: Hungarian Rhapsody No

♫☆ Chopin: Nocturne No

♫☆ Debussy: Suite bergamasque, CD 82, L

♫☆ Bach, JS: Jesu, Joy of Man's Desiring

(from Cantata No.

As stunned as I was, I was not satisfied.

It's a hobby. Shopping for clothes and school

supplies makes me happy. I must feel an

emotional connection.

I found myself gliding to the back of the store

where the music sheets led me. They were all

aligned and displayed on the wall: in different

colors, sizes, and fonts. The last music sheet

had fallen off the display, just like a poster

slides off a wall and onto the floor. It skated

its way over to the "no pile" that the lady

invisibly created.

The lady smirked.

I had curiously picked it up and read it.

There was no song title, no artist, no lyrics.

It was blank!

"Excuse me, miss?" I asked.

"No, NO, nope, EH this is broken. Why would I sell it?" she threw some items over her shoulder.

I don't think she heard me.

"Miss, excuse me, I have a question," I said a little louder.

"Yes, uh, gimme a second; I am a little busy, dear," she snickered.

I waited for what felt like 10 minutes.

I started tapping my foot on the floor.

She looked at my foot, then my face.

She looked at my face, then my foot.

Then she proceeded to say, "Yes, how may I help you?"

Before I could answer, she let out a faint gasp.

"Oh yes, yes, I wondered when you would come by," she said out of breath as she twisted her head analyzing me like a specimen.

I looked at her, confused.

"I was going to ask you what piece of music this was? It caught my attention, and I wondered if you could tell me a little bit about it?"

"You are the one," she whispered, elongating every word. Her eyes and eyebrows lifted as she said that.

"You know what to do," she whispered slightly louder.

I checked the price on the display, and it said $0.

I asked another question.

"Okay, so then is this free of charge?"

She nodded and vanished behind her cluster of junk.

I left the store confused but oddly fulfilled.

I waited outside for my chauffeur to show up.

It started to rain.

I liked the rain.

It was as simple as that.

Rain makes me happy, just like music.

I let out a gasp created by anxiety as I

remembered what I had been holding in my

hand, in the soaking wet rain.

The music sheet!!

Chapter 3

❧

A Surprising Outcome

I looked down at the paper and mentally

envisioned what I would see—a soaking, wet,

unrecoverable, torn, yellow (ish) piece of

paper.

"Huh?" I said out loud.

It was good as new!

I felt so relieved.

I looked down again.

"Huh?" I had said it even louder than the first

time.

All of a sudden, I saw musical notes forming.

There was a dotted half note and then the
eighth note.

I let out a long "woAHH."

I was so confused.

How could this be possible?

Well, I bought it (not really) with no writing
on it.

All of a sudden, the title and words started to
appear!

I thought to myself...

No, this could not be Latin or Arabic? It looks
Greek, maybe?

Oh my, what could this possibly be?

I concluded that it was no language. It was
just an elementary school kids doodle
....I think?

I was at a loss for words.

The chauffeur honked at me three times and proceeded to roll down his window.

"Hey Constance, are you okay? I have been here for three minutes honking and waving."

"Yes, I am fine, sorry, just a little tired, that's all."

The door shut, and the lights dimmed.

I closed my eyes, and before I knew it, I was fast asleep.

A bump in the road shook me awake.

I blinked several times as I came back to reality, and realized I was almost home.

The chauffeur made his usual jokingly snarky comment.

"Good morning, princess," he mimicked in a little girl's voice.

As soon as I got home, I rushed to my piano.

I couldn't tell if that adrenaline stemmed from joy of not having to speak with my annoying chauffeur, or being able to play a fresh sheet of music.

Whatever it was, I was happy.

I took a deep breath, placed the piece of paper on the stand, set my fingers on the keys, and closed my eyes.

"Here we go," I said.

As I opened them to read what was on the paper, I realized I had been staring at the paper I had initially purchased.

It was blank, again.

I was shocked.

Shocked was not even a word qualified enough to describe what I, CONSTANCE ANDILET, felt.

What the heck.

Literally.

I let out a burst of anger.

Then I let out another burst of frustration.

A light bulb just turned on in my head.

Water.

Rain.

That is what had uncovered the black and gold ink!

It was still raining!

I went out, took the blank paper, and let it soak.

Not even a drop of water was absorbed into the paper.

It was as if it was water-resistant.

I pretended not to look at it.

I acted as if that would do something.

I was desperate to understand something ununderstandable.

Nothing changed.

No lyric or musical note appeared.

HAH, what is this!!!!

I chuckled.

I went back inside and stared at the paper.

Out of frustration, I ripped the paper into six pieces.

I threw it in the trash bin and called it a day.

Waste of $0, I muttered under my breath.

STUPID, FLIPPING THING!!

UGHHAHAAH.

My jaw remained clenched the entire night.

Chapter 4

❧

The Following Morning

I woke up to the sound of birds chirping and the fireplace crackling. The house maids always lit up the fire around dusk till the late morning.

November in Leonthuria was like spring in the North Pole. It was always cold. Fall and Winter. Winter and Fall. The colors would change. The leaves would crisp. Then the wind would whistle through the streets. And finally, the snowflakes would fall. The snowflakes would droop down in the town, from flurries to snowflakes. Leonthuria winters would be covered in inches and inches of snow. The town would dance around the communal Christmas tree. Each year people would gather, throw snowballs at each other, and make the tree together. Christmas music is playing through invisible speakers. It has always been magical. This year however, looks different, alot different. The town is suffering. Mamma and Papa have been struggling to maintain peace with the citizens of our country. The town looks upon us to feed the people, but we do not have food to give away. We need it for ourselves, or we will soon run out too. People are dying of hyperthermia. As sad as it is, my family needed to think about ourselves.

My family nor I are the bad guys. The saying "family first" applies to our situation right now. So I do not blame myself. Why should I? Reader, you must agree; I mean, just put yourself in my shoes.

I removed this thought from my head and continued to sleep. The sounds of the fire crackling created a calm ambiance. I fell asleep in a matter of seconds under my cozy wool blanket.

I heard a familiar voice say, "Constance, you need to wake up now!"

"Mhmm," I grunted.

"Wake up, hurry!"

I opened my eyes and saw Anastasia.

"Anastasia, what are you doing here? You

scared me," I said as I put my hands beside my legs to position myself up.

"I need to show you something," she whispered.

She sat at the edge of my bed.

"Anastasia!! Stop; why are you being so serious? Wait-how did you even get in here?" I questioned.

She glared at me and took out a camera.

I stared at her expressionless, pale face, and looked at what she had been showing me.

It was a video of mamma and papa.

I panicked and thought that they were in trouble.

My heart started beating faster.

It was a video of them walking along the lake they always walked at.

I smiled.

This was the lake where they said "I do" to one another.

I have photos upon photos of their wedding.

People praised them like no other.

Their wedding was viewed and seen by more than 1,000,000 people.

As beautiful as it was, I was tired.

"Anastasia, why would you wake me up for this? You know my beauty secret is beauty sleep, duh," I muttered as I jokingly pushed her shoulder.

The Christmas tree that was across the lake had been knocked over.

I gasped.

I positioned myself closer to the camera.

My jaw dropped as uncertainty arose.

The lights were flickering.

Children were crying.

Motionless people on the floor.

Screams had emerged from behind the camera.

A stampede of people with torches marched and burned down chanting.

"Selfish, worthless people. How dare you, Dutch and Dutchess, not feed us in times of need. Shame on you. Today you will learn your lesson," the people harmonized.

The camera swooshed over to another angle.

My mom and dad stared at each other with
fear.

They proceeded to apologize, shouting in
sorrow, shaking.

A man amongst the herd of people threw junk
at my terrified parents.

That shut them up.

A man shouted, "Today you will learn."

One hundred people synchronized the chant,
"Today, you will learn."

They all sprinted towards mamma and papa.

The man behind the camera dropped on the
floor, and the footage flatlined.

The remainder of the clip was on a black
screen, in which the only image I saw was the
reflection of my terrified face.

"Are they okay, Anastasia, please tell me they

are okay?" I asked with a quiver in my voice.

"No, no, they must be!" I sobbed.

"How could this happen? They did not do

anything?" I asked with a shaky voice.

I looked at Anastasia expressionless.

There was no answer.

"ANASTASIA!" I screamed

I grabbed her shoulders and shook her in

hopes of her answering me.

"WHAT DO YOU KNOW, YOU MUST TELL

ME?" I shouted in the hope of receiving an

answer.

"I am sorry, Constance, I do not know what to

tell you. I have not heard from them."

Chapter 5

&

Magic?

A finger wiped a tear that was followed by another, and another. Anastasia looked me in the eyes and nodded. I didn't know what that nod meant or if it needed to be translated into words. I just knew that a nod like that meant something. Whether that was an "everything is going to be okay" nod, or a "you'll figure it out" nod, I accepted it.

I heard the door lightly close. The creaking sound augmented as the door grew closer to shutting. I stared blankly--at nothing.

Feeling light-headed, I positioned myself,

with my two hands behind my back

supporting me, slowly sliding my way to lay

down in bed. My left hand then touched a

wrinkled paper. I gasped as I was still in

shock but realized it was only paper.

I took a deep breath and turned my neck over

my shoulder, and I glided the paper to the

side of my hip, and finally moved it in front of

my eyesight.

The linens of my mattress did not permit me

to do so easily.

I gasped again.

But this time, I gasped in fear, surprise,

shock, and confusion.

I breathe heavier and heavier as my eyes look

up from the parchment and start frantically

pacing in all directions as if that would somehow resolve my confusion.

I-

I-how is that possible? I attempted to ask myself.

I am at a loss for words.

A million thoughts were running through my head.

It was almost like when you think you're going crazy, but you are still sane and aware that you are not crazy yet.

The tears had flooded my bed and wet my skin.

I took another deep, shaky breath, and came to a conclusion.

The music sheet that I had ripped into six pieces had become one, and it was in my right hand.

The metallic gold song sheet was as light as a flashlight. The light bounced off in all directions and shone in the dark room I was in.

Another tear dripped slowly down the corner of my eye, to the left side of my nose, drooling down to the bottom of my chin, and dripped onto the paper.

 The tear spiraled down the paper, and as each teardrop landed on the paper, a ball of light would appear.

The words and letters slowly started to appear one by one.

Before I knew it, there it was again; a legible,

beautiful sheet of music.

With no doubt in my mind, I rushed to the

piano.

I sprinted to the elevator but realized it was

five floors down.

The piano was located on the third floor.

I decided to use the stairs, and in the process,

I would be burning calories too!

I ran to the piano; I took a deep breath and

glided my fingers over the keys.

One-two-three-four.

La -la -dah-mm-duh-ra.

The music produced by the keys was unusual

but enchanting.

The dizziness got worse.

The music continued.

It got stranger and stranger.

Something that I have never heard before.

It felt so proper and correct.

Almost like being in a Porsche Cayenne and

having the seats hug your body.

It was too perfect.

I closed my eyes and kept pressing the keys.

I opened them as I felt a floating sensation.

The keys were glowing white, and my fingers

became slowly invisible, dissolving into each

note that I played.

My pinky started blending in with the keys,

then my bracelet, then my arm, then my

whole body suddenly melted into the keys of

the grand piano.

The melody continued.

La -la -dah-mm-duh-ra-.

La -la -dah-mm-duh-ra.

Ah AAh AAAAH.

Before I knew it, I was in the midst of

nothing.

Nothing.

Nothing was to be seen.

Indeed I was not on the third floor of my

house.

Or in my bedroom

Or in the ballet room

Or in the grocery store

Or in my closet

Or in my--

Okay, you get the point.

I was in a white cloud.

Perhaps I died?

I had no clue.

And to be honest, I just wanted to wake up

and call all this a nightmare.

Chapter 6

&

The Terrible Sighting

A loud ringing sound woke me.

Awoke is a big word; let's call it "barely made me open my eyes."

La -la -dah-mm-duh-ra.

La -la -dah-mm-duh-ra.

This melody interchangeably played along with a ringing sound.

The voice of two kids laughing filled my ears.

A boy and a girl.

My eyes had been opening and closing inconsistently.

I saw all the colors: red, orange, yellow, green, blue, purple.

Finally, no more white.

Until the laughs filled my ears again.

I became in touch with reality again.

I was slanted sideways.

I blinked several times to focus my eyes on what I was seeing.

I was on the dirty floor with a puddle under my left foot.

A couple of hair strands near my eye and mouth.

And I saw something I had never expected to see.

A family of 8 holding hands, circulating the Christmas tree.

The one that everyone helps put up in

Leonthuria.

This was home. I was home.I was safe.

But how did I get here? I asked my

subconscious.

The family crossed their hands in a swinging

motion, rotating in a circular motion around

the tree.

They were singing the melody.

La -la -dah-mm-duh-ra.

The same melody I had played on the piano.

An angelic female voice singing followed it.

Ah, AAh AAAAH.

At this point, I had itched my head, gotten up

from the floor, and remained criss-cross

applesauce on the floor.

I had moved those annoying strands of hair from my face.

My eyes squinted in the process.

If what was going on was an expression, my face would be the perfect expression to use.

The song, the setting, uh, am I dreaming? I asked my subconscious again.

No answer.

This time I wanted to hear answers, listen to words, and take advice.

I did not care if it would bore me or not.

I just wished someone could sit down and explain everything.

I looked down at my legs, and I noticed I was wearing stockings.

I was wearing beige pants.

For the record, I never wear pants and stockings.

Talk about no fashion sense.

I looked horrid.

The thought of my appearance made my heartbeat beat faster and faster.

I immediately bent my neck down to gaze over and analyzed my clothing.

"Athena….Athena….where are you?" a woman cried.

I felt a hand on my shoulder.

"Athena, what are you doing here?" the lady mentioned.

"I have been looking all over for you!" she cried again.

I looked at the lady as a stranger and flicked her hand off me.

"UM, who are you, and why are you touching me?" I said in a disgusted manner.

"How dare you speak to your mother like that. Athena, go to your room," A man who was out of breath yelled.

I looked at him and said, " I am not Athena, I AM CONSTANCE ANDILET THE SECOND, AND MY PARENTS ARE THE DUTCH AND DUCHESS OF LUTHERIA. LEAVE ME ALONE. YOU HAVE THE WRONG PERSON."

I had lost my temper.

Who were these people?

If they wanted to play games, today was the wrong day to play them.

My so-called parents looked at each other in shock.

Then back to me.

Then at each other again.

"Sweetie, now how hard you hit your head?" the lady curiously asked.

"OH, THIS IS ABSURD," The man chanted.

I was grabbed by the wrist and dragged into a one-story wooden house.

The wood splintered my skin.

The stranger dragged me.

I proceeded to scream, but nothing came out of my mouth. I was shocked, utterly shocked.

I was then dramatically let go of next to the moldy bread.

"EWWWWW, clean your house; this is disgusting," I muttered.

"You have the nerve to speak to us like that, huh? What has gotten into you? This is your home. This is your house. We are your parents. I do not want to hear one more word from you. Enough is enough. Go to your room," the man said as he pointed toward the corner.

Shaking, I got up and followed the direction of his finger.

I was led to a moldy-smelling twin-size bed. I looked at it in disgust.

I sat there motionless, counting the number of times I blinked in a second.

I was disrupted by this intricate hobby as I heard murmuring.

The family that was so-called "mine" were crying.

I was shedding tears.

If there is one thing I cannot stand, it is when people cry obnoxiously.

Like, I get it you're sad, but like, get over it.

What am I supposed to do? I cannot help but laugh. Sorry, not sorry.

The conversation attracted me, partially because this junk of a cabin was so small that all I could hear was their voices.

I got up on one knee, and my foot followed.

I stabilized myself and used my hands to help me stand up.

In my head, I screamed with joy as I scanned the room and noticed a mirror.

Before I had fully gotten up, horror got the best of me, and I fell back down.

I had scared myself.

The sight of my reflection was unrecognizable.

Not because my face was in the dirt but because it was not me.

Literally.

Talk about terror.

I stabilized myself again, shuddering my breath, and got back up.

I rushed to touch my face and hair.

I felt the oil on the skin the mirror displayed

and prickly hair.

OKAY, side note, whoever's body I was in is

clearly three months due for their botox and

hair appointment.

Talk about depressing.

Confusion simultaneously filled my thoughts.

I pondered how on earth this could be

possible.

Now I am really starting to question if I hit

my head.

A tear dripped down my cheek, my skin

absorbing the liquid.

I could not stop.

Until a loud sob followed another, and then

another

I am afraid I startled the people around me

as they ran toward me in distress.

Chapter 7

&

Awoken In A Strange Reality

The sound of pots and mugs clinking had awoken me.

It was a beautiful day with the birds chirping.

"Athena, sweeettttieee," a lady called.

I decided to get up and walk over to where the voice is coming from.

"Yes," I replied.

"How are you feeling?" she said with a smile, yet concerned look.

"I am feeling so much better, thank you!" I exclaimed.

"Breakfast?" she asked in a muffled manner as she proceeded to stuff her face.

I made a disgusted countenance, hoping she would get the message that I was not interested.

"Honey, you know times are tough now; we cannot afford to eat other meals," she remarked.

"Huh," I uttered.

Like, I don't know what is going on in life. To be honest, I am just yoloing.

"TIMES ARE TOUGH," I mimicked bitterly.

Like what? I don't even know where I am.

The last thing I need is food being taken away from me.

Food=happiness.

"Athena, clearly you are still not yourself; go sit in the corner," a man demanded.

"Uh- excuse you, I have sat in that minuscule corner next to the toilet for hours. I refuse to sit there until nighttime, thank you very much," I stated as I looked down at my nails in desperate need of a manicure.

"Athena, I cannot even believe you right now. Do leave at this very instant. Come back before I wake up tomorrow and figure the rest out. Goodbye," the lady ordered.

I gladly left and even made sure to flip my hair in their faces before leaving, or so I attempted.

This hair was not flippable as it was prickly and not silky-smooth.

I had at least tried to make my dramatic exit.

At that point, I had just kept walking and
rethinking my thoughts.

My body subconsciously did the walking
while I did the overthinking.

You see I have always been good at
multi-tasking.

I had zoned and dazed out a few times here
and there.

Until I became in touch with reality again.

There I was.

I was in front of the dirty floor, viewing the
Christmas tree.

I was in front of a different family who
crossed their hands interchangeably, and
sang the song:

La -la -dah-mm-duh-ra-.

La -la -dah-mm-duh-ra.

Ah, AAh AAAAH.

Dizziness consumed my thoughts.

Until I saw another girl next to me, crying, on

the floor.

I looked at her as if she had three eyes, and

she looked at me as if I had four.

I stood up while she was lying sideways in

the dirt, with mud all over her face.

A strand of hair fell between her lips, and her

saliva started to drool.

As she laid there, I continuously spectated.

Curiosity was not even my primary intent for

staring.

Every move, everything she had done, I had done before.

AS IF THIS COULD NOT GET EVEN WEIRDER. I wanted to throw a tantrum!

My fists clenched as I heard another voice, though this one was unfamiliar.

"Penelope, where are you?" a little girl would call, hoping to receive an answer.

Her voice grew louder and louder as she arrived in the vicinity of our location.

The girl in front of me used her hand in the back to stabilize her getting up.

Just like I had done!

At that point, she had zoned me entirely out.

She looked at the ground as her eyebrows lifted while she pondered.

You could tell she was thinking about 1,000 things per minute.

"Penelope, there you are! Where have you been?" a little girl asked as she touched her hand on her shoulder.

The girl, startled, moved away.

"Who are you, why are you touching me, ew; UGH, I hate this," the girl complained and questioned.

I looked at her and said, "spoiled little brat."

I looked back at the little girl and said, "aha, who does she think she is? Anyhow you have a goodnight; good luck dealing with her."

As I laughed and shrugged it off, I continued walking.

This time I led one foot in front of the other, conscious of where I was going.

Until it occurred to me that I had been just like that girl.

"Who was she?" I asked myself.

Chapter 8

8

Infatuated

"Are you new to this?" a handsome, tall, brunette boy asked.

I looked around me as if I had gotten in touch with reality again.

He was everywhere.

I could see him but three times in three different directions.

I did not know where he physically was; all I knew was that he was attractive, had a pleasant voice, and was not visible.

"YOUUUWHOOOO," he said as my vision came back to me.

I had been so overwhelmed by everything

that had been going on that I was going crazy.

"Hi, sorry, who are you?!" I asked flirtatiously.

With crossed arms, he leaned on a Japanese

blossom tree and laughed.

I gazed at him in a confused manner.

All jokes aside, why is he like this? I don't

find it funny. I miss being at home; I realized

that I couldn't command people to do

anything here; it is as if they command me.

"HELLOOOOO, am I talking to a wall?" I

said in a more harsh voice as I walked closer

and closer to him.

He cleared his voice.

"Hey, hi, hello. So I am Evander; let's keep it

at that."

"Well, hello, Evander. I am Constance Andilet," I breathlessly said.

"Out of curiosity, who on earth would name their child Evander?" I questioned expressionlessly.

For the second time, he cleared his throat and whispered, "the thing is, Ms. Andilet, they didn't."

I smiled as I squinted my eyes.

No one referred to me by my last name unless they were referring to my father about political matters in Leounthuria.

"Well Evander, if I am not mistaken, means "man of courage" in Irish. Let's just say that the Irish history 101 textbook taught me that," I smirked.

He chuckled.

"Ms. Andilet, I am afraid your Irish 101 textbook didn't teach you very much, considering Evander means "good man" in Greek. Nice try, though," he said as he sarcastically gave me a thumbs up.

I looked up at his charming smile and golden-brown hair.

"Oh, shut it. We both know I am smarter than you," I awkwardly remarked.

My cheeks turned red.

"Ooh la la, is someone nervous now, Andilet?" he asked

The pink flower from the Japanese Cherry Blossom Tree had landed right on his left cheek.

Perfect timing, I said in my head.

"Ooh la la, is someone blushing now,

Evander?" I said as I pointed to his face in a

french accent.

Confused, he looked behind him, then back at

me, and said, "what-"

I walked up to him, swooshing my fingers like

a magical wand, and plucked the flower off

his cheek.

I grabbed his right hand, opened his fist, and

placed the flower on his palm.

As I patted his hand shut, I smiled and said,

"See you around, Mr. Evander."

I skipped along the tree, where the people

had taken a break from dancing around it.

Smiling, I let out a chuckle.

Minutes passed by, and I could not stop thinking about him.

I let out a long sigh as I saw two swans in a lake glide.

All I could do was think about his tall figure, his light-brunette hair, his blue eyes, his clear-tan skin, his amazing pearly-white teeth, and should I continue?

I admitted to myself, I think I have a bit of a crush-

No, stop it, you don't.

Okay, no, I do.

Andilet, no, you don't.

Woah, WAIT, why did I call myself Andilet.

Wait, EW, why am I even talking to myself?

That's so weird-

I took a deep breath and realized that the

whole last name thing was catching on.

I never liked my last name, but he made me

like it because all I could do was think of him

saying it in his mocking, flirtatious way.

Chapter 9

Confused

I picked up some flowers from nearby the
lake and danced my way back to the
one-story house.

Now that I was in a good mood, I felt I could
do anything.

Literally.

I could even pretend that those strangers
were family and that I was Athena.

After all, Athena was quite the cute name.

Suddenly a shock of terror hit me.

Did Evander see me as Athena or Constance
because the last time I looked in the mirror, I

suffered severe PTSD. My hair was untamed;

my clothes were ripped.

Oh dear god, how could he ever like me-

My best friend Anastasia told me that it is

not all about the looks.

Maybe he thought of me as funny, or I don't

know.

Anastasia shut up, stop overthinking

everything you loser, I told myself repeatedly.

I continued skipping, and I inevitably ended

up on the porch of my so-called "parents."

I put on a smile that neededn't be put on

because I was delighted, TRULY.

I knocked on the door four times because four

is an even number, therefore it's good.

"Mother" opened the door and, without emotion, looked at me awaiting a response.

"Hello, mother, I had some thoughts about our conversation earlier this morning, and I wanted to apologize."

Mid-sentence, a smile grew on her face. She wiped her sweaty-muddy hands on the dirty apron and motioned me to come in.

Before I stepped foot inside, I looked down at the flowers and said, " I know these may mean far less than my actions, but I thought a flower or two may brighten your day and allow you to accept my apologies."

Her smile brightened even more, and before she could speak in joy, a man's voice interfered.

"Athena," a low-pitch voice said as the man shifted the door open.

I looked him in the eyes, his unique, genuine, watery eyes.

That was my so-called "father."

He continued, "...I am so proud of you. You demonstrated growth today. We know your personality, and clearly, we have spoiled you with love, so we are happy that you realized you were in the wrong on your own. I don't know what happened to you these days, but something did. I am just so proud that you are back to your usual, bubbly, kind-hearted self. The girl that we raised you to be. You know that actions speak louder than words, and by doing this, we forgive you."

Mother chuckled.

I smiled, and I too had watery eyes.

"Thank you, thank you, thank you," I said as I ran to tackle them both with a hug.

Once wrapped in their arms, I blinked several times, staring at the chipped wooden floor.

I realized I had never really been hugged like that before.

I embraced that emotion- that empty, yet fulfilling emotion in my stomach and heart. Some say that feeling is love, and it can only be found in fairytales with significant others. But this, this feeling was different. I felt my inner child, my little 6 year old self safe, and that is a feeling I will never forget.

Many people like to romanticize the life of royalty, but, you know, my family is still a family at the end of the day.

So with such a fantastic title, I receive such little attention from my true mother and father.

As the circle of hugs loosened up, I backed three feet with tears in my eyes, and I thanked them.

Confused, they looked at me and decided to appreciate the happy daughter they thought was theirs and smiled back.

The birds chirped and sang a familiar song

that awoke me.

Aware that this family of mine is living in

poverty, I knew it would be a miracle to find a

clock in this one-story house.

I tried to put my astronomy class where I

would take the time to do my hair and have

my nails painted to use. I tried to estimate

the time of day.

Due to unfortunate circumstances, or in

simpler terms- a lack of paying attention in

class, I could only understand that I was awake before sunrise.

You know, I get it...paying attention is not everybody's strong suit. So I advise when confused as to what hour of the day it is, to just look outside at the sky:) I know not many people know that, but it helps, alot!

After all this math and intellectual work, I decided to get up and take a stroll around the lake that I skipped around yesterday.

As I closed the wooden door shut, a nail bolt clanked on the entryway corner, making a rather unpleasant sound.

That wasn't the only thing that made my jaw drop by surprise that day.

Amid this chaotic morning, I had been humming "Tchaikovsky Swan Lake Music." This was the perfect song, in my opinion, because I knew how to play it on the piano and dance to it during ballet practice.

I knew every "hum" and "aaah" by heart. The nature in this land that I like to call "Idontknowtopia," was filled with strange, magical species.

The swan near the lake the other day was white with gold markings on its wings, and it floated within these two golden, circular hoops.

One hoop was vertical, and the other was horizontal, so they intersected in such an artistic way.

It connected to a beautifully sculpted golden

crown while the swan gracefully laid in the

hoops, floating, and flying over the lake.

The hoops would skid over the water, making

a light, splashing noise.

Aside from this beautiful, strange animal, I

bumped into a lovely little creature.

NEWSFLASH, that was what startled me

that morning.

They call it The Pink Mockingjay.

LITERALLY, think of the hot juicy couture

era kind of pink.

I was amazed.

No silly, not by the color, but by its talent.

As I had hummed and hummed and

continued doing so, when I reached the

outdoors, I realized that they were singing

the Tchaikovsky Swan Lake Music.

I couldn't help but drop the nail bolt I picked

up from the door and dance.

I turned, twisted, leaped, and even went on

my tippy-toes!!

The beautiful birds followed me as I glided

through their homes.

They grew louder and louder until the end of

the song that I hummed approached.

I decided to make a grand ending, so I did a

triple spin, and I landed in a split.

*** totally not on accident.

Hundreds of birds went quiet in a matter of

seconds.

That was not the only thing that went quiet.

I had landed in the wrong position, tearing my pants.

I sat there shocked, a little in pain, and allowed my expressions of dramatics to kick in.

Before I could get up, I heard a familiar voice.

I felt the presence of a person behind me.

I couldn't tell who, but whoever it was, better not have seen that embarrassing fall.

"Need a hand," a man said.

I turned my head in the direction of the voice.

I immediately jumped up, crossed legged, and put my hands over the tear above my knee.

"Oh, it is you, Evander!" I said with relief and excitement.

Until I realized he had probably seen it all.

Before he could reply with his usual witty comment, I stopped him and asked "oh, please, please, please, please tell me you did not see that last part."

He chuckled and said, "Ms. Andilet, I am so sorry to inform you that I do not have any coinage in my pockets because that fall was worth paying for. Talk about free entertainment."

He chuckled even more.

I shoved his shoulder and sighed, shrugging it off.

"You know, Evander, I feel that you were following me. What are the odds you happened to be here right at this hour, where I am," I jokingly interrogated him.

"Hmmm, props to you for noticing, Ms. Detective Agent. I hate to rebuttal your observations and inform you on a very factual thing," he responded.

"And what is that very factual thing," I said in a confused but smiley manner while elongating every word.

"You see, Andilet, I was erem, walking and taking a morning stroll, you know, fresh air!" he said quickly.

He hastily quickened his steps.

"And it is because of these reasons that your accusation no longer stands," he confidently remarked, raising his eyebrows with pride.

"WOAH, Ahh, WOW, I must say I am impressed," I commented in a flabbergasted manner.

"How long did you practice that cover story in the mirror, Evander," I questioned.

"Looks like I owe you my dearest apologies for concocting such accusatory claims," I said as he unfolded his arms.

"Ummm, I must say, though, that through this huge, major coincidence, seeing your beautiful brown, wavy hair blow in every direction as you danced truly made my day," he said as he romantically gazed into my eyes.

"HOLD ON-" I blurted out loudly.

"What, Constance, did I do something

wrong-" he anxiously said.

Anxious about what response I may receive, I

questioned, "BROWN HAIR?"

"Oh god, Andilet, seriously. You scared me. I

thought I said something wrong. Oh, dear

snickerdoodles in Candyland, give me back

my sanity," he pleaded to himself on his knees

dramatically.

I approached him closer, anxiously begging

for a response.

I asked, "No, WAIT, can you see my brown

hair???"

"YESSS, it is so beautiful!" he said as he

played with it, twirling every strand.

"But-" I muttered.

"But in the mirror, I see a girl with tangled blonde hair, dirty skin, terrible fashion sense, and nails in desperate need of a manicure! What is it that you see?"

"I see a beautiful girl that is working on herself for the better, who has the heart as big as a lion, talent that will take her far in life," he positively ranted.

My eyes fluttered as I heard the compliments that had been said.

"That truly does mean a lot to me, you have no idea, but I was asking physically! What do you see? I don't mean to alarm you, but in the other land I come from, my name is Constance Andilet; I have brown hair, ocean blue eyes, olive skin, pink-pretty nails, you get it...I was fabulous! Do you see that description, or do you see what I see in the mirror," I asked.

"Well, no. I see parts of what you described in your homeland and parts of what you described in the mirror; I see beautiful brunette hair, but hazel eyes; I see a mixture of olive skin, and fairer skin; I see the hands of a woman who cannot afford to maintain them, and another hand with smooth, gorgeous skin/nails," he breathlessly said.

He continued, "I see lips that speak words of kindness, but eyes that have the capability of judgment."

"I am soooo confused," I replied.

"You see, before I spoke with you under that Japanese Blossom Tree, I saw Athena, the girl you described. But each time I made you laugh, you stopped with your snarky comments, your appearance changed back to your true self, Constance Andilet. And I hate to misspeak, but I think this Idontknowtopia is rewarding you, piece by piece, bit by bit, every time you improve on yourself," he kindly whispered.

"I am afraid I don't understand," I seriously whispered.

"Why do you think you are here, Andilet? Why are you being called "Athena" by some strangers?" he questioned.

"I-"

Stuttering, I finished my sentence.

"I am afraid I dont know that either."

I looked at the grassy floor in pure puzzlement.

"Well, you are new here, Ms. Andilet," he smiled.

 "That's why I am here, that's why you are here, that's why everybody is here. We are all guilty of being spoiled, cruel, rude, and cocky. Some may even call us brats. Now I don't have all the answers, but from what I have gathered, this Idontknowtopia, as you say, is teaching us a lesson and giving us a second chance that we do not have in the real world" he paused.

I motioned him to continue…

"Being spoiled in a land made up of suffering is a big crime. Athena, the girl you are stationed to be, is a girl who loves her family very much but struggles to live. Her family eats once a day while you, I, him over there, have more food than we could ever consume…"

He patted his belly jokingly.

"I think," he said as I took another deep breath.

"I think you were put in her shoes, Athena's, to experience poverty with your own eyes. And each time you become more open-minded, you understand that not everyone has your life. People like me, see you, piece by piece..." he took another long, deep breath.

"You see, when I first met you, I saw Athena. When I started getting to know you, I saw scraps of you, the true you, not some spoiled girl that doesn't think twice about a word she says. So I think that if you keep doing what your doing, your skin tone will emerge, your eye color will turn blue, your soft hands with long-polished nails will be pink," he concluded.

"So if I am what you say I am, and if this situation is what you say it is, what could you possibly be doing here considering your name translates to "good man," I asked.

"You know Evander isn't my real name; it was when I became a good man," he said seriously.

"HAHA very funny ev ev," I laughed as I patted my thigh to mimic utter laughter. I gulped my warm saliva, which reproduced at an abnormal rate due to the confusion I had just endured.

"No, seriously, it used to be kakomathiméno paidí!" he shamingly commented that that translates to spoiled brat in Greek.

"My parents foreshadowed the reason for their demise, and when they had me, the spoiledness was already in my veins," he said.

"Woah Woah Woah, let me get this straight, I know I made fun of your parents for calling you Evander, or so I thought, but really,

"spoiled brat?"

 I laughed even harder.

I muttered, "looks like they got creative; my

applauds go to them."

He pushed my shoulder to shove me away in

disapproval of my hilarious joke.

I skipped back "home" with a smiley

countenance and greeted my pretend parents.

"Why are you so cheerful?" the mom

questioned me.

"Haha, can I not smile and be happy?" I

laughed with a curious undertone.

I had just surprised them with fresh bread

and flowers that I worked for in my spare

time.

I was so happy to see their expressions as
they received this rare gift not just from me
but from the world in which they live, their
reality.

As the evening approached, I overheard "my
parents" discussing this beautiful castle.

I was intrigued to hear the imagery and
descriptions of this beautiful mansion.

Living in this condition, you forget any form
of luxury seen in any previous life.

Hearing the domes and statues that
decorated this abode made me drool.

Until I heard them talking about the people
who inhabit this place.

I paused, expressionless, and tears fell down
my cheek.

I have never felt more empathy for the people whose home I inhabited.

They were describing me, the real me, Constance.

That was the house that I grew up in.

The way they described the spoiledness and ignorance of Constance shocked me.

I hadn't realized the importance of perspective and how I was living in a completely different world, planet even.

I hated myself and who I had become.

That was my house that overlooked the country of Leonthuria.

Or was that just an illusion?

Or is this character I am playing simply going ill?

I instantly remembered what Evander had told me.

Maybe I was sent here by fate to pay for my actions....

I stayed up, looking at the stars, disturbed.

The night passed, and so did my sadness. I took the time to reflect on who I wanted to be.

I have always been given a choice to choose; I have always had things handed to me, quite like bubble sheet answers.

Funny right! Never having to discover who I am, and what I like creatively. What the answer is to so many questions.

I got up as soon as I heard "mom" scream.

She was pointing at the hand in, which was utterly destroyed, and bloody.

Apparently, she came back from the cotton mills factory late at night, and "dad" tried to disinfect it.

She had passed out from the pain and had awoken in that instant.

I was speechless.

"Dad, " told me to call anyone, even a stranger for help!

I stood there frozen, unable to process what was going on.

The muffled screams and cries went in one ear of mine and out the other.

He got up, shaking my shoulders, asking again, getting blood all over my shirt in the process.

I awoke from my shocked daydream and ran
for help.

Running over the broken wood and opening
the creaky, glued-on door, I yelled,

"HELPPPPP, ANYONE HELPPPPP."

Strangers peaked through their windows and
doors.

Some imitated the confused daydream I had
earlier.

Others came to help.

My "father" explained what happened, and
luckily one neighbor had experience as a
doctor.

He sanitized the arm, bandaged it, and made
her a treatment soup.

He mixed different herbs and scents.

This would act as a temporary sedative and tranquilizer.

He pulled over my "dad" aside and explained what would happen.

"It's not looking too good, man."

"Okay, but please, what can we do? There must be something," the loving husband pleaded.

"I suppose the only thing to do is wait, have her rest, and eat."

I rushed over to the corner I slept in and sobbed quietly.

I couldn't believe what had just happened.

I felt so bad, so guilty for everything that had happened.

I didn't even have the decency to ask what she did during the day when I went to pick flowers and occasionally work a few minutes for a slice of bread.

"Oh, stupid me," I said, nodding my head in agreement with my thoughts.

Stupid me.

...

Several days passed, and I noticed we were limited with food.

"Dad" starts rationing his slices of bread for "Mother."

I gave my scraps of bread to him and told him to eat them.

A few minutes later, I kissed his hand, saying everything would be okay, and told him I would be back soon.

I paid a visit to the cotton mills.

Now that "mom" stopped working, and "dad" had to look after her, I forced myself to do the right thing- work.

I needn't even need an introduction as the head of the cotton mills factory grabbed my hand.

He yelled, "CHILD, what are you doing relaxing? Get to work!"

I took a deep breath and looked at the other workers around me.

With some observation, I got to work and fit in right away.

We were paid at the end of the day with a basket of bread.

I did this for several weeks and, on occasion, saw Evander.

He applauded and counseled me throughout all this.

I couldn't have been more grateful for such a good man like him to be near me.

He was like the light at the end of a tunnel, a precious thing to look forward to talking to.

After seeing him, I would go to my "parents" and check up on both of them, feeding their weak bodies.

After what felt like a couple of months, food was becoming increasingly more difficult to obtain given the economic state the village was in.

I had started to give my darling family the scraps I would find – starving myself effectively demobilizing, yet I did so happily. After all I didn't mind losing a few pounds:)

It was then when I said the words "I love you," and this time, I meant it. They have done so much for me, even though I was their so-called "daughter." I wanted to make sure they knew how grateful I was.

"Mother" got much better as the infection started to heal on its own.

Life was getting back to normal, except for one change.

My spirit.

I grew to be more loving and understanding.

Using my humor to bring the smiles out of

the hopeless faces that worked every morning

starting at 5:00 am with the only thing

displayed on the hands of these workers was

not gold, bright jewlery, rather dirt under

their nails.

I was forever grateful for this growth, and I

looked forward to challenging it every day.

Bettering myself for other people, but most

importantly for myself.

It gave me a sense of closure.

Quite like a scab on the skin that never heals

and always reopens.

I felt that that scab started to turn

permanently into a scar.

I shared this thought with Evander, and he said something sensible.

"Don't be afraid to show your scars," he whispered into my ear.

I pulled back my head gently to look him in the eyes with a wider perspective, pupils dilating, and took my final breath before I made a remark.

"Why? They make me look weak," I said in a quizzical voice.

"No, they show how strong you are," he argued as he held my head with both his arms reassuring me.

"How?" I asked eyes squinted, awaiting a response.

"Because you have survived what the Devil
threw your way every day," he replied.

I wish I could frame this discussion into a
piece of art on my wall.

For me the devil wasn't the classical figure
with horns, it was what I saw in the mirror.

It was myself, my selfish self.

This hit every bit of my subconscious that
thought differently, negatively, and wrongly.

"You are so wise, Evander; I hope you know
that," I said as I brushed through his hair,
playfully shaking his head.

Bending down, I kissed him on the cheek,
right where his beauty mark was, as he laid
there on my legs, in the grass, near the lake.

The scenery overlooked the forest with all of

its beautiful creatures.

He looked me in the eyes and caressed my

face, playing with my hair.

The birds chirped in sync with our chuckles.

Moments passed in harmony were

unfortunately scheduled and time limited.

We had walked home to both of our "families,"

and played pretend once again.

Chapter II

&

The Mysterious Whisperer

"Psssst," a young man whispered.

"PSSSSssst," he whispered a little louder.

I awoke from my sleep, somewhat confused.

I looked around to find the source of where

the voice was coming from.

"Andilet over here," a familiar voice said.

A smile consumed my face when I realized

who was speaking; I just didn't know where

he was.

I tip-toed outside, trying not to wake up those

around me, and Evander greeted me just

outside the door.

"Hi, what are you doing here," I asked in joy, as I wrapped my arms around his neck.

"I came here to say goodbye," he said.

I took a couple steps back slurring my words as if I have spent the night before drinking my sorrows away.

"Goodbye? No, why are you leaving? Where are you going?" I interrogated in a hopeful tone.

"As much as I don't want to leave this magical world, I am afraid my time has come, Andilet," he said, "I truly am sorry."

"-though the only thing I am sorry of is leaving you," he continued.

"Why do you have to leave, and why can't you stay here," I argued as I took a step forward to where I was earlier.

"I came here as a man full of malice, wrongful pride, and hubris. I now leave a much better man and am ready to prove to my parents, and those around me wrong. I have changed. I couldn't thank you enough for helping me do so, for now is the time I go back home," he sighed.

I remained there expressionless and processed what I had just been told.

The one person that made the things that made no sense make sense was leaving.

I had no one around me that understood me as he did.

He glanced at me and placed something in my right hand, lifting each finger from my surprised fist.

I looked down and saw a flower, a beautiful flower.

He explained that that was the same flower that fell from the Japanese cherry blossom tree when we first met, and how I must keep it beside me as a constant reminder to be a good person.

I chuckled and let out a cry.

"Thank you for everything you have done," I said joyfully.

"No, thank you, Ms. Andilet, or should I say, Constance," he said as he turned his back and walked away.

Each step he took further away pained me.

Three minutes passed, and I decided to catch

up to his footsteps.

He was at the tree, with all the children

circling him singing.

La -la -dah-mm-duh-ra.

They continued

Ah AAA Ahh

They harmonized, encircling him; he saw me

standing there and blew me a kiss.

In less than a second, he was gone.

I couldn't believe it.

I was all alone.

I asked myself if I would ever see him

again...

I replied to my own thoughts answering this very question.

Well, maybe in another lifetime.

Hopefully.

Three months passed since Evander left.

My favorite thing to do when I wasn't helping

the community or my family was sitting

under the beautiful Japanese Cherry Blossom

Trees.

If I were ever conflicted or feeling like I was

going back to my old ways, I would pretend

like Evander was there.

He helped me become a better version of

myself, and I couldn't thank him enough.

The rest, though, was up to me.

A person can help you buy the pieces to a puzzle and start it, but you have to be the one to complete it with the final pieces.

The days were spent in joy, and Penelope gave me loads of company as I did her. She was no longer the "new girl," she was a friend.

I told her everything about Evander!

She came to me for advice and just a general understanding of why exactly we were here.

She and I talked about our lives back home and never really understood poverty because we were always immersed in glamour and wealth.

We would often spend hours talking about a variety of things.

One day we were teaching the kids in the village how to dance, as Penelope did competitive ballet for seven years, and I did it my whole life.

"Have we met before?" I asked her

"Well, no, I dont believe we have," she said.

"Oh-okay, never mind then. You remind me of my best friend back home, and you almost sound like her too," I remarked with a laugh. She giggled.

"Well, that's odd; I have a friend back home that reminds me of you. However, the odd thing is that you are quite the opposite of her," she professed.

"How so?" I questioned.

"Huh- I can't put it into words, but you just

are," she said.

We shrugged our shoulders to signal our

favorite slang term, "WHAT EVA."

It's our new thing.

It's the thing.

Everyone did it too.

We then resumed the dance lesson and

shared several laughs with the villagers.

We were interrupted by a stampede of angry

adults who stormed the city near the tree.

They marched chanting slurs in the form of

protest.

Penelope and I looked at each other as if we

had seen a familiar sighting.

Immediately the villagers grabbed our hands

and rushed us near the decorated tree.

They were encircling us before we knew it,

singing and harmonizing over the protest and

chants.

La -la -dah-mm-duh-ra.

They sang louder

Ah AAA Ahh

The kids mouthed the words "thank you" as

they began to blur from our vision.

Visions of Penelope, the kids, the voices, and

my old bedroom intermingled unexpectedly.

The screaming, singing, and protesting

sounds stopped when I awoke in my bedroom

with Anastasia.

My head threw itself off my pillow as if I had just awoken from a fever dream.

Before we could even speak, we looked at each other with a sight of terror.

Confused more than ever, we pinched our skin to see if this was all real.

"Did you-"

"Did we just-?"

There was a pause.

"What just happened?" we said in sync as we raised our voices, confused.

After sitting there with our thoughts gathered, we realized that we were both in a magical world, and we came back.

We were let out because we changed, and now we must spread kindness and help those in need.

"Gosh, I am so happy to be back in my skin and flesh," Anastasia sighed with relief.

"No way you were Penelope?" I exclaimed as I moved away from her in shock.

"Woah, you were Athena?" Anastasia exclaimed even louder, doing the same motion.

We were so relieved to be back to normal.

"So wait, can we just talk about what happened, and EVANDER, is he real?" a million questions exited Anastasia's mouth.

We laughed in the name of our delirium.

All was well until we caught sight of what was happening.

The yelling and shouting we heard minutes before returning home had started again.

We stood up, trying to discover and locate the source of this noise.

It was outside, right where we were with the villagers.

We witnessed a sight of terror.

"My parents…our parents….our family-" I shouted.

They took Anastasias' parents too.

Anastasia frantically got up as I did when I "awoke" previously.

We need to do something; we cannot let them become hostages of mad villagers.

Whatever it is they want, we must give it!

We stormed down the stairs, disregarding the luxurious elevator, and walked to the ledge overlooking the villagers.

The built-in speakers near the ledge acted as a megaphone when standing at the right angle.

I ran out of breath and overlooked the village.

The particles of the gravel I had run over dispersed into the air, and danced back down slowly.

I blinked several times, analyzing what was around me.

I cleared my voice, and began...

"My fellow people, I am here today to apologize. I am here to apologize for my actions and my wrongdoings. I understand why you are mad. I understand why you have this boiling hatred that consumes your every action. You are famished and left to starve when people of noble birth like me are overnourished with all the luxuries in the world! I am here today to say that your voice has been heard," I spoke proudly as my voice cracked toward the end.

Several angry protesters looked up to listen more attentively, simultaneously pausing what they were doing.

I gulped loudly, anxiously awaiting a positive response.

My eyes stared at the villagers' left to right, back and forth.

I swallowed the saliva that built up in my mouth, and prepared to speak again.

"For weeks, I have understood the importance of perspective. I grew up in a world where the only perspective I reflected on was my own. The only stories I chose to listen to were those I wanted to hear. You see the world is made of more than money and yachts. Our rich hearts and open minds pay for any expense due," I declared.

"And that is why I am here to open the doors of my house to any visitor. That is why I am here to feed everyone with feasts. That is why I am here to ensure that every person is gifted a luxury of their choice. With this being said, please, end this gruesome battle and protest right here and right now. Let us become of one status and not many. After all, we are all the same," I said, catching my breath.

"We all do a little happy dance when something goes right, we all cry of laughter when someone makes a joke, we all enjoy being positive."

I continued, "We all lose hope, we all fight our own battles, and we all contemplate if life is worth living. You see we are all the same. Let anyone and everyone remain happy and content with life, afterall we only get to live it once."

Anastasia smiled at me in admiration for what I said.

Slowly but surely, every protester dropped their weapons.

The metal and torches clanked as they hit the floor.

My eyes followed the sounds of the weapons falling, and the people who dropped them.

"We are all here for a reason. We are given a choice on how to act and portray ourselves. It is the choices we make that reflect our true character. Thank you," I concluded.

In admiration of the crowd, I awaited, saluting each individual in awe.

Each villager who chose to salute me met me halfway, and we both walked up to each other.

This proves there is no hierarchy.

This proves that we are all on the same level,

regardless of status, wealth, or background.

After all this socializing, I took the flower

outside my pocket. The one that Evander

gave me, and kissed it.

I held it up on the ledge as if it were a hard

fought trophy, and said that this flower

represents the eternal peace this community

will maintain.

I turned my back listening to my thoughts,

and looked back at the gravel that once

fought natures gravity.

Evander, You would be so proud.

I am sure of it.

...

Anastasia and I were back with our parents,

and life resumed. The villagers were happy,

and everyone was content with their lives.

Often times I would walk past the villagers to

help them with their needs.

I passed the beautiful house where I once

stayed and glanced at the loving family that I

temporarily got to be a part of.

I saw the beautiful, kind-hearted, genuine

Athena.

The family I got to say hello to every morning

looked so content.

As I stared into the window of the

disintegrating cottage, I felt a presence

behind me, and quite a familiar one.

I smelled a masculine scent that captivated

me emotionally, making it hard not to spoil

the surprise.

I did my little happy dance internally as I

imagined who was behind me.

"Hey, nice speech out there, Andilet," a male

voice said

I gasped.

"Oh, Evander!!!" I exhilarated.

He was right under the Japanese Cherry

Blossom Tree, waiting for me.

He let his arms out as I jumped into his arms.

He lifted me into the air and looked me in the

eyes.

The rest was history.

♥-♥-♥-♥

About the author

Hi there, reader ♥
*My name is Allegra Vercesi, and I am a
sixteen-year-old girly girl in my Sophomore year of
high school. I have two loving parents; both born and
raised in Italy. I was born in Lake Como, and I grew
up in Dubai for eleven years of my life. This book
incorporates elements of my fourth-grade imagination
to the current one I have today. I ultimately live
writing analytical essays for classes, speeches, and
debates on current affairs. Sometimes, however, I
forget to dive into my creative magical fantasies. I
always enjoyed flipping through the pages of books as a
child that co-shared principles of intriguing stories yet
imperative moral lessons. There is nothing more
refreshing than finishing a book satisfied- the feeling of
flipping the last page, eyeing the final paragraph, and
reading the last word with delight. That is the goal of
my book. It is truly a dream come true that I am able
to publish my first book at sixteen. I hope you enjoy
this good read and get something out of it <3*

Much love,

Allegra Vercesi